The Last Supper

Basque Original Series No. 27

The Last Supper

Gabriel Urza

Center for Basque Studies
University of Nevada, Reno
2021

Basque Original Series No. 27
William A. Douglass Center for Basque Studies
University of Nevada, Reno
Reno, Nevada 89557
http://basque.unr.edu

ISBN: 978-1-949805-58-1

Library of Congress Cataloging-in-Publication Data
Library of Congress Cataloging-in-Publication Data

Names: Urza, Gabriel, author.
Title: The last supper / Gabriel Urza.
Description: Reno, Nevada : Center for Basque Studies, University of Nevada, [2022] | Series: Basque original series ; no. 27

Identifiers: LCCN 2021056543 | ISBN 9781949805581 (paperback)
Subjects: LCSH: Basque Country (Spain)--Fiction. | LCGFT: Novels.
Classification: LCC PS3621.R93 L37 2022 | DDC 813/.6--dc23
LC record available at https://lccn.loc.gov/2021056543

The Last Supper

It is only today, in her university office on an afternoon in early November, that Julia learns of Xabier Etxetoa's death by suicide in Sestao, a suburb of Bilbao in northern Spain. A "today" that is also, coincidentally, the day of the American presidential election, though Julia wonders whether this is coincidence at all or whether both events—Xabier's death and the candidacy of the television star—might simply be the reincarnation of an old familiar force reaching out beyond the grave and across the Atlantic to once again exert itself.

With the news of Xabier's suicide Julia has allowed herself to lose sight of the election—the television's red and blue graphs, its manic talking heads. It isn't expected to be a close contest, and both the newspaper columnists and her fellow university faculty members have assured her that by midnight on the West Coast the specter of the television star will be banished forever. She has been active on campus for these last four months, ever since the television star secured his party's nomination, and so she feels that she deserves this reprieve. She is the faculty advisor for several progressive student groups—the Greens, the campus chapter of NOW. Her evenings and weekends have been consumed with student rallies and protests, with fundraisers and voter registration drives and phone banks. Her office in the Department of Anthropology is strewn with flyers and posters photocopied in the department copy room after hours. But because of her confidence in the election's results, and because of the weight of the email she has just received, she has decided to forgo the various parties scheduled to celebrate the television star's defeat in order to sit alone with the news of Xabier's death.

*

Julia is still alone in her office at eight when her daughter, Katie, calls from New York.

She thinks, initially, that the connection must be broken, her daughter's voice cutting in and out, before realizing that there is nothing wrong with the connection—her daughter is crying.

When Julia hangs up the telephone a few minutes later, she grasps for the first time what had so recently been inconceivable: that the television star may, in fact, be her next president. She sits, stunned, at her desk, then begins to type the name of a news site into the search bar of her laptop. She stops herself, however, before the page can load. Outside, from the front steps of the university's library, she hears the shrieks of young voices, the pop of fireworks, though she can't translate the sounds. Are they in protest of the election's arriving results, or in celebration, or simply the everyday noises of a university? She folds the computer closed, unable to bring herself to read the headlines proclaiming the television star's victory, the surreal image of the man's face beneath a stream of ticker tape.

Instead, Julia finds herself returning to the email informing her of Xabier's suicide—sent by a mutual friend in Pamplona who had come across the obituary. Grief, she thinks, is at least an emotion that is grounded in reality.

As she reads the email a second time, she realizes that she hadn't been surprised by its contents—only that it had been so long in coming. She has been expecting the news for nearly forty years now. In the time since Julia first met the two young Basque priests in 1968, the same year of their arrests, she has often wondered whether what had happened after their meeting was truly a miscalculation. Or whether Xabier and Josu could somehow have predicted all that would become of them afterward—their incarcerations, their torture, even Xabier's suicide now—and chosen it anyway.

It's late, nearly ten, when Julia finally gathers herself to leave her office. The campus has been unusually empty all evening. She's the last faculty member to be found in the department; only a late-night custodian and a few exhausted graduate students passing occasionally in the hall remain. Julia's office teems with a career's worth of books on Basque Nationalism and the Franco dictatorship in Spain, bowing the bookshelves lining the small room. In the corner of the office, behind the door, sits a gym bag filled with damp workout clothes—she's recently begun attending an aerobic bicycling class between lectures—and along her desktop are a few pictures of her daughter's family: At a lakeshore in the Adirondacks. At her granddaughter's first birthday party.

I should head home, Julia thinks, before reminding herself that no one is waiting for her there. Katie's father and Julia had divorced while Katie was still in high school, and though Julia has dated since—a few times seriously—she's never remarried. Clearing stacks of graded essays off of her desk, Julia now tries to remember Xabier as she met him that first night in Don Eugenio's apartment in 1968, not as she knew him after forty years of correspondence and familiarity and history. It is a memory so distant, so discordant with what she has come to know, that she remembers it as if recalling a book she'd read long ago: a loose collection of images and plot points, a story whose meaning Julia has long since forgotten. Her life has remained tied to both Xabier and Josu ever since that first meeting, but she is always astounded to realize that the night at Don Eugenio's apartment was the only time that all three were ever in the same room together.

The two events of the day—the election and the news of Xabier's suicide—begin to meld together, to inform one another, and she is visited by the unsettling feeling of living through history for a second time. She gathers a few papers from her desktop, then turns off the office light and closes the door behind her, trying to unpack the déjà vu she now feels, the sense of entering, suddenly and unwittingly, into a world that has been set free of logic, into a reality that could be dictated by the whims of a wizard behind a screen.

*

It was in August of 1968 that Julia first met the two young priests.

They had arrived, unannounced, at Don Eugenio's apartment in Santutxu at just after ten in the evening. At the sound of the door buzzer the old professor had gathered himself from the fraying Wembley rug where he did his reading, sweeping a few longer strands of hair over a balding forehead as he started toward the door.

"I wasn't expecting company," he said.

Julia shrugged, making clear that she hadn't been waiting for anyone either. The evenings devoted to reading and study had become routine since her first night in Don Eugenio's apartment in Bilbao three months earlier, though it wasn't uncommon for visitors to stop in for a glass of wine or a coffee. Lourdes, the Basque woman who also lived in Eugenio's apartment, cracked the front door uneasily as the door buzzer sounded once again, pressing an eye to the opening. Julia had observed this cautiousness before—caution that bordered on paranoia. *What does a university professor have to fear?* she had wondered. But now, upon seeing the door buzzers on the other side, Lourdes swung the door wide.

"*Chavales*!" Lourdes said. "How long has it been? In, in."

It was the first time she had heard Lourdes use slang, and there was a lightness in her voice that was foreign to Julia. Lourdes had always been friendly, but was careful to keep a distance between the two of them. It served to remind Julia that even though she was welcome in Don Eugenio's apartment, she was still a guest. But with the arrival of the two priests, this barrier now seemed to fall away effortlessly, without resistance. Lourdes ushered the young men into the apartment the way someone might welcome grandchildren who had stopped by unexpectedly. The men—both, like her, in their early twenties—watched Julia as they leaned in to kiss Lourdes once on each cheek before entering the apartment.

"Ah," Don Eugenio said, shaking his head. The priests had apparently given no advance notice of their arrival, but Don Eugenio seemed unsurprised when Lourdes shuffled from the entryway with Xabier Etxetoa and Josu Juretegia in tow. "The young firebrands I was telling you about."

"*Gabon*, Don Eugenio," said the younger looking of the two. He began in Basque, but switched abruptly to Spanish. "And this is the famous American that you mentioned?"

"She speaks *euskara*," Don Eugenio told them in Basque.

"I understand pretty well, anyway," Julia said. She'd been studying the Basque language intensively for five years—since a semester in San Sebastián during her undergraduate studies—and by now she spoke fluently. But it was her practice to keep expectations low; most Basques were surprised simply to learn that a foreigner had taken an interest in their language, which had been outlawed by Franco a decade earlier. Proof of proficiency was only an added bonus.

The first of the young priests put out a hand, his wide smile revealing a gray, dead incisor. He was dressed in American-style blue jeans and a collared shirt with the sleeves rolled to his elbows, a tangle of dark curls above two thick eyebrows. Julia would never have picked him as a priest. A bartender, maybe, or even a primary school teacher. He exuded a youthful energy that bordered on childishness, and when she shook his hand he grasped her arm eagerly.

"Don Eugenio has told us a lot about you," he said. "We can't express how grateful we are to have someone from the United States interested in our cause."

Julia felt Don Eugenio stiffen momentarily at the mention of the word "cause," before prompting Josu forward for an introduction.

If Xabier had seemed overly youthful, then Josu Juretegia gave Julia the impression of being older than his years, possessing an intensity that would remain for the next four decades of their friendship. His black hair was cut short and severe, and his thin hand was cool and powerful as it reached out from the sleeve of a navy sweater. He introduced himself stiffly, revealing very little, and if Don Eugenio hadn't earlier told Julia that he had only been out of seminary for a year, she would have guessed him to be a decade older. As Julia felt Josu inspecting her, she simultaneously noticed Xabier sniffing comically at the air, moving slowly down the hallway toward the kitchen, past two large oil paintings by Jose Luis Zumeta.

"Is that . . ." He paused, turning towards Lourdes theatrically. "Are those *pimientos verdes* that I smell?"

Lourdes smiled shyly, pulling down the sleeves of her sweater as she nodded. Don Eugenio's face glowed with delight at the sight of Lourdes' fidgeting.

"And tell me, do these *pimientos verdes* happen to be from the town of Gernika?" Xabier continued.

"*Bai*," she said weakly, nodding again.

"And is it true what they say? That the sweetest, greenest, most flavorful, most succulent peppers in the world are grown in a town by the name of Gernika, which happens to be the town that my mother was born in, where I myself was raised into the handsome young clergyman before you today?"

Lourdes' neck flushed. She seemed young and bashful in a way that Julia had never before seen in her months living in the apartment. When Don Eugenio agreed by letter to sponsor Julia's summer of thesis work in the Basque Country, the professor insisted that she stay in the spare bedroom next to Lourdes' in the flat he had inherited from his father, a wealthy industrialist, before the war.

Lourdes' exact connection to Don Eugenio was unclear. She was twenty years his junior, and might have been a cousin, or a niece, or the daughter of a friend, or perhaps something more or less than any of these options. Their relationship would remain a mystery even after Julia returned to Spain for Don Eugenio's funeral a decade later, when Lourdes was consoled at the casket by a procession of university professors and administrators the way a widow would have been.

"A stroke," Don Eugenio had said when he introduced Julia to Lourdes on her first day in the apartment. The left side of the woman's body sagged downward, causing her to cradle her left arm in her right and to drag her foot slightly when she walked. Lourdes had smiled as if in apology, the left corner of her mouth remaining motionless. Don Eugenio had continued to speak as if Lourdes weren't standing there in the room. "She was only thirteen when it happened. Her parents weren't in a position to take care of her—she came straight here from the hospital."

But with the arrival of the two priests, Julia noticed that Lourdes' limp seemed to dissipate, her posture straightening even as she blushed at Xabier's playful flirting.

"Would you gentlemen like to join us in the kitchen for a pepper or two?" Don Eugenio finally said, sparing Lourdes from the attention of the young priest.

"Well," Xabier said, already walking towards the kitchen, "if you're going to insist upon it, what choice do we have?"

*

Two weeks before the election of the television star and Xabier's suicide in Spain, a young woman had stopped Julia outside the lecture hall after class. Julia recognized the girl from her seminar on the antecedents of the Basque independence movement in Spain—the girl struck Julia as smart but overly idealistic, a typical campus radical who spent her weekends organizing protests against the World Trade Organization and multinational oil corporations. She dressed almost entirely in black, her clothes and backpack littered with sewn-on patches that announced what Julia could only assume to be band names.

"I've been meaning to ask what you think of all this," the young woman said. "Of the election, I mean."

Julia had been expecting a question about the lecture she'd given that day, or perhaps a request for a letter of recommendation. Despite her role as faculty advisor for student groups actively campaigning against the television star, she wasn't used to being asked so explicitly about her own politics, and the question at once felt intimate and transgressive. The young woman flipped a wisp of dyed green hair behind her ear, watching Julia expectantly.

"Are you asking who I'm going to vote for?" Julia asked. She thought she saw the young woman's eyes roll momentarily.

"I'm assuming I *know* who you're voting for," the young woman said, flashing a conspiratorial smile. "I mean, what do you *think* of all this? Given your work on fascist regimes like Franco's." She gestured to the empty classroom, as if it contained Julia's three books, her four dozen articles, her boxes of field notes. It was as if this single question, this simple gesture, made real a sentiment that had been lingering in Julia's subconscious for some time now.

"I haven't really thought of it in that context," she confessed.

There was a long pause, as if the girl were disappointed in her answer.

"It's terrifying," the girl said finally. "Have you seen the rallies? The way he speaks? The lies?"

Julia nodded. It was a realization that she'd come to recently: the television star had become so popular *because* of the boldness of his dishonesties and indiscretions, not in spite of them.

"Well, I'm looking forward to it all being over in a couple weeks," Julia said, trying to bring the conversation to a close.

"But what if he wins?" the young woman pressed. "What if it *isn't* over in a couple weeks? Considering your work in Spain, don't you worry about what might happen?"

Julia noticed a copy of her first book, *A Dictator's Truth: Reality in the Era of Franco*, on top of a stack under the girl's arm.

"It seems different," Julia said, shaking her head.

But even as she said this, she wondered if it was true. When she had arrived in the Basque Country in 1968, she reminded herself, Franco had already been in power for nearly three decades. She hadn't been there to see the transition, the national slide toward a lethargic acceptance of the tiny general's warped worldview. How one man's reality could take hold of a country.

*

That first night, the four of them had settled in around a small table in the corner of Don Eugenio's kitchen—Josu leaning back against the white tiles of the far wall while Xabier drew his chair in close between Don Eugenio and Julia—as Lourdes busied herself at the stove. Xabier immediately began to ask about Julia's work in the Basque Country. From his questions she got the impression that Don Eugenio had described her work as being in support of the nationalist movement that had sprung up in the Basque Country in the past decade.

In reality, her research had focused on tracing the origins of American Basque immigrants back to their family homes in Spain, but she said nothing to contradict Xabier's idea of her work.

Don Eugenio began in on the political situation in the Basque Country under the *Caudillo*, as he disdainfully referred to the dictator. Franco's *Guardia Civil* roamed the worn cobblestones of small Basque towns, the professor told her, breaking the noses and ribs of young men for saying the wrong thing—sometimes for just *thinking* the wrong thing, it seemed. For having an idea in the wrong language.

It was as if the *Caudillo* had personally stomped over the anonymous graves that had been filling since the close of the civil war in '39, said the professor, so that even the craftiest of dissident ghosts would remain trapped underground. By that summer of 1968, Franco's regime had already eradicated old dances such as the *Jota* from each town's annual fiestas, and the voices of dissidents such as José Luis Alvarez Enparantza and Julen

Madariaga had been silenced either by prison bar or by bullet.

But even this hadn't been enough for the *Generalísimo*, the self-proclaimed Unifier of Modern Spain, Don Eugenio said. The dictator's paranoia led him to safeguard not only against the threat of *present*-day Basque—and Galician, and Catalan, and Romani—dissidents, but also against dissidents past and future.

"Did you know, Julia, that our benevolent dictator has developed the ability to travel across time?" he asked.

He explained how Franco had already outlawed the Basque language, creating a generation without speech—a generation that couldn't even understand the language of their parents or grandparents. But now, Don Eugenio said, the *Caudillo* had begun traveling to the future in his quest for a Basqueless nation, declaring that children would no longer be given Basque names, and so Ibons became Juans, Patxis became

Franciscos, Mirens became Marias from that time onward.

It was a fanciful metaphor, this idea of time travel, and one that had delighted Julia that first night. She'd thought it an elegant comparison, one that brilliantly captured the absurdity of life under Franco, where reality was always skewed just a few degrees off-center, where people were either "friends of Spain" or its enemies. She could see why Don Eugenio was such a popular professor, why he seemed to walk in a wake of admiring young political science students whenever he was on campus.

"In addition to his Basqueless future, the *Generalísimo* has even begun to create a Basqueless past," Don Eugenio continued. He described how Franco's men had recently been entering cemeteries in the dark of night to chisel Basque names away from old headstones, so that whole towns woke to discover their parents and grandparents and great-grandparents no longer possessed last names, and the living could no longer be sure that they were related to the dead at all. He replaced the highway signs to ancient towns such as Donostia and Gasteiz so that the roads from Madrid now led to new Spanish cities named San Sebastián and Vitoria.

"It's true," said Xabier, his eyebrows raising comically. "Just last week I went to the graveyard in Sestao to visit my parents. All this time, I could have sworn that I was a Basque, that I had Basque parents and a Basque last name. It turns out I've been wrong this whole time. The headstones proved it."

He shook his head in mock disbelief. Don Eugenio smiled sadly.

"I went home and tried to write a letter to my brother in Deba, but that same day the *Caudillo* informed me that the Basque language no longer exists. Now, I can't even write my brother to tell him he's not Basque. Can you imagine?"

Don Eugenio patted the young priest on the shoulder, seemingly pleased with the anecdote. The professor then uncorked a bottle of *cosechero* that he had taken from under a kitchen counter, continuing with his history lesson while the young priests nodded in agreement.

"It's to a breaking point," Don Eugenio concluded. "You can sense it everywhere you go."

"I remember people saying that the last time I was here," Julia said. It was true; during her last trip two summers before, people were already talking of an armed resistance. Graffiti had appeared on the walls of the old part of town, carrying menacing slogans against the Regime.

"A lot has changed in two years," he said, holding his hands open in front of him. "There's more talk of organization now. The Guardia Civil raided a *baserri* in Deba a week ago and confiscated twenty kilos of explosives found under the floorboards in the kitchen. And you've seen the reaction to the death of the boy in Errenteria."

Three months before, a young militant named Txabi Etxebarrieta had been shot dead by the Spanish Guardia Civil as he fled from a roadblock near the French border. Julia had read about it in the *Tribune* on the flight from Chicago to La Guardia on the way to Paris—a single bullet point in the World News section of the paper offered without context or comment—but when she arrived in the Basque Country a week later she had found conversations steering, with slow inevitability, towards the young ETA member's death.

"And you?" Julia asked Don Eugenio. "Have you managed to stay clear of the bombs and the bullets up at the *Uni*?"

She had meant for it to lighten the mood—Don Eugenio had taught political science at Deusto, a Jesuit university in Bilbao, for nearly thirty years. He'd become an institution there despite his lectures against the Catholic Church's support of the Franco regime, which had earned him the nickname "The Liberation Pedagogist." During Julia's first week in Bilbao that summer, a literature professor at the university had pulled her aside to warn against being too closely associated with Don Eugenio. *Trouble follows him*, he had said. *He invites it upon himself.* But the literature professor was prone to melodrama, and she'd thought little of his warning.

"You joke, Julia, but the students have become much more involved," Don Eugenio said. He paused as if considering whether to add whatever would come next, which was a habit of his. The group sat quietly, waiting for him to continue.

"But it's what's happening within the Church that's the most interesting," he said finally. He nodded towards Xabier Etxetoa and Josu Juretegia. "This is where you should be concentrating your investigations."

"And now the Church has become as much of a problem as the *tocapelotas* from Madrid," Xabier said, looking to Don Eugenio for validation.

"Don't forget who you are, Xabier," Josu said suddenly, his first words since they had sat down at the table. Don Eugenio nodded his head in agreement with Josu. "You're a representative of the Church, for at least another day anyway. And a priest doesn't speak that way."

"What?" Xabier said, still smiling broadly. He shrugged his shoulders innocently. "Are you telling me that our Supreme Commander, our Dictator-in-Chief, our Director of Oppressive Cultural Services, is not in fact a *tocapelotas*? That he has not, in fact, touched the balls of another man, or of many other men?"

"Xabi, enough." Don Eugenio spoke sharply. "Listen to your colleague. If you expect to keep any of the respect your position deserves, you need to stop speaking like a steelman."

This was, in fact, not an unwarranted admonition; both Xabier and Josu had spent the last year working at a steel mill outside of Portugalete, Don Eugenio explained to Julia, along with a handful of other young clergymen who had recently graduated from seminary. They had done so—rather than simply accepting a parish assignment—after learning that the salaries of the parish priests, and of the bishop himself, were paid straight from the pockets of the *Caudillo*.

"Bah," Xabier said. "It's different now, Don Eugenio. People aren't stuck on the image of the clergy as much. What's important now is action."

The old man shook his head again, as a father might shake his head at the exploits of a young son—equal parts disapproval and admiration.

"What's the Church, if not symbolism?" he asked absently. He looked Xabier up and down, then regarded Josu. "But symbolism and action don't have to be mutually exclusive."

Josu nodded pensively in his corner, while Xabier tore off a chunk of the baguette that Lourdes had placed on a cutting board on the table.

"Well put, Don Eugenio," Xabier said. "We couldn't agree more, actually. Right, Josu?"

Julia turned in the direction of Josu. The young priest seemed to wither at the attention, his face flushing in a way that betrayed his youth for the first time.

"Go on," Xabier urged. "Tell her."

Josu looked first to Julia, then to Don Eugenio.

"It's all right," Don Eugenio said. He put a hand to the back of Julia's neck, squeezing gently the way her grandfather used to. "*She's on our side*, Josu."

Julia nodded, not knowing what exactly she was assenting to. She was beginning to realize, for the first time, the ignorance in which she'd been living for the last few months in Don Eugenio's apartment. She recalled the stories that she'd heard about people being arrested for merely grumbling about Franco and his regime, about how they disappeared into police stations and courtrooms and never returned. She wondered what information was concealed within the walls of the aristocratic fourth-floor apartment in Santutxu, who exactly was hiding behind the academic façade Don Eugenio had presented for the past three months. All of these things at once, and still she nodded, urging Josu Juretegia to go on, to include her in their collusion.

The young priest sipped from the glass of wine that Don Eugenio had placed in front of him.

"That's what we wanted to talk to you about tonight, Don Eugenio," he said reluctantly, regarding Julia again. "I understand what you are saying. We were hoping that we could speak to you in private about a certain matter."

The heads at the table again turned in Julia's direction; even Lourdes seemed to be watching now as she placed the first bowl of green peppers on the table. The peppers shone an earthy green beneath a sheen of hot olive oil, crystals of sea salt clinging to the withered skins like small diamonds. In the pause Julia could feel Don Eugenio once again considering her, as if he were coming to a decision over a question he had not fully thought about until that moment. But it was Lourdes who spoke.

"You can talk to her as if you were speaking to me," she said. They were her first words since they'd moved to the kitchen, and Julia was surprised that Lourdes had been following the conversation.

She tried to catch her eye to express her thanks, but Lourdes had removed herself from the conversation as quickly as she had entered it, reaching up on her good leg for a serving dish on a high cupboard shelf.

"Of course you can," Don Eugenio said. "She's a friend, Josu."

Josu studied her for another moment, as if trying to decide whether Don Eugenio had said this merely for his guest's benefit, or if she could truly be trusted. But before Josu could come to a decision Xabier folded his hands and leaned in conspiratorially.

"A hunger strike," he said.

*

Julia had planned to attend a victory party held by the progressive student organizations on campus, but now the scene at the student union would more likely be funereal, even dangerous. There is a palpable tension in the air as she makes her way to the parking garage from her office in the Anthropology Department; the few people she crosses paths with on campus eye each other suspiciously, as if feeling one another out, trying to gauge the others' allegiances, whether they had voted for or against the television star. The other candidate, the politician who had played by the old rules, has already ceased to exist. Now it is only those for and those against the television star, and she feels the people around her trying to establish who is in which camp. She is aware, for the first time in her home country, of the small features and details that might be used to deduce allegiances. The clothes she wears. The car she drives. The place she works.

There is, of course, a sense of safety on campus—the demographics of a college campus in a liberal state are on her side—but as she merges into traffic she feels unsteady, more vulnerable. At a stop light a mile from campus she hears a horn blaring behind her, and in the rearview mirror she sees the headlights flashing on an older sedan. A young man hangs his head out of the driver's side window, waving a large blue banner emblazoned with the television star's name. Julia remembers the bumper sticker on the back of her car, with the logo from the defeated candidate. The man in the car yells something from the window, the unintelligible words rimmed with self-satisfaction and anger.

The man's outrage, his idiotic flag waving, reminds Julia not of the television star—though the similarities are obvious—but rather of a rally in Madrid when she'd first arrived in 1968, where Franco loyalists gathered in front of the Ministry of State Security in the Plaza del Sol, holding up placards of the General's soft, effete face. *He seems like a clown*, she had thought at the time, before she knew better.

Perhaps that's what had seemed so familiar about the television star: his buffoonery, the grotesqueness of his persona. In the newspaper photographs of Franco, the tiny dictator would be clad ridiculously in fur cloaks, or in a meticulously pressed military uniform that gave him the appearance more of a child in costume than of the man who had done the unexpected—led a military coup that had deposed a democratically elected government and had maintained control of Spain for thirty years. By 1968 Franco had already become a caricature of himself. Outlandish. Almost performative. Not unlike other strongmen since: Castro with his cigar, Gaddafi's gold sunglasses, Chávez's red beret.

"The Great Ventriloquist," Don Eugenio had once called Franco, in a way that merged disgust with admiration. He'd used the term to capture the dictator's ability to speak through bishops and judges, through prosecutors and prison guards. And yet, on this night in November in northern California, Julia now feels the television star speaking through the man in the car behind her, his horn still blaring, the stoplight still red. She wonders what other mouths the television star is already communicating through, what might come next. In the man's blaring horn Julia feels the accretion of the television star's powers, and she wonders how he might next upend her reality.

The light changes to green and Julia puts the car into gear. The cars around her thin, and she hears only the scream of the man's engine as he passes her, the flag with the television star's name whipping in the beam of her headlights before disappearing into the night.

*

Josu's plan was uncomplicated. He and Xabier would arrive in their priests' cassocks at the front steps of the bishop's private residence the next morning, where they would simply stay in silent prayer and protest. Josu had already been reprimanded several times by the bishop for sermons denouncing the Church's support of Franco, so while there would be no formal declarations, no public display of purpose, it would be understood by their previous activism in the Church that their hunger strike was in reaction to Franco's systematic repression of Basque identity, and to their Church's support of the *Caudillo*. A hunger strike was unheard-of in Spain, but it followed in the tradition of peaceful protest that had been propagated worldwide by social and religious leaders such as Gandhi and Martin Luther King, Jr., who had been shot in Memphis earlier that spring. Josu and Xabier had come to Don Eugenio to ask him to serve as an intermediary, to contact the local media during their silent fast and to speak on their behalf.

"We've been discussing something like this for a while now," Don Eugenio said. It was an odd thing to add; the statement seemed to be addressed only to Julia, as if he felt a need to take ownership in the young priests' plot. "It's the perfect way to force the Church to acknowledge its involvement with the Regime."

"So you'll do it, then," Josu said to Don Eugenio. Julia felt that this was a final question to a debate that had been ongoing for some time.

"I don't think I'll be much help to you, I'm afraid," Don Eugenio said, spreading his hands across the richly embroidered green tablecloth. "On your way over to the apartment, you noticed,

I'm sure, the young man with the light overcoat lingering across the street, smoking a cigarette?"

Neither of the young priests responded. A palpable quiet settled over the kitchen, interrupted only by the popping of oil in the iron pan over the gas burner.

"He's been there ten hours a day for the past three weeks," Don Eugenio finally continued. "Since my speech at the Academia de Bellas Artes. And when he's not there, he has a couple of friends who take his place."

Julia watched the two priests turn toward the wall where the professor pointed, as if they could see through it and out into the street on the other side of the salon. She pushed back her chair on the white tile flooring, carrying her wine glass with her as she walked into the salon and opened the glass door leading onto the balcony four stories above the street. Josu followed her out of the kitchen, stepping behind her to slide to the opposite end of the balcony. In the apartment building across the street, children were silhouetted by black-and-white television screens in living room windows; a man read the morning newspaper at a kitchen table while his teenage daughter rinsed dishes in the sink. Julia leaned out over the railing, peering down into the dark street.

In an entryway below was a dark shape that she couldn't be sure was even human, until the small red circle of a cigarette tip glowed in the shadow, just as Don Eugenio had said. The wine glass shivered lightly in her fingertips; she was embarrassed by her naivety, but also felt betrayed by Don Eugenio for not disclosing something as important as this, something that could jeopardize her own safety.

"It's like this now," the somber young priest said. "You think Eugenio is exaggerating about the situation, and you're probably right. But I'd bet my life on it—this is the beginning of something serious."

They stared out into the night, both lost in their own thoughts. In the apartment building across from them a light suddenly came on, illuminating a bedroom. Clothes hung out of a dresser drawer, and an ashtray on the nightstand spilled over with white cigarette butts. A middle-aged woman entered the bedroom in bare feet; Julia watched the woman lean over to slide down her pantyhose, then fall back limply on the unmade bed. A man followed into the room, a glass of amber liquor in one hand.

"We should go back inside," Julia said, but neither of them made a move toward the apartment. It was suddenly too late; they had passed an unspoken point of intimacy without realizing it. The man was kneeling now between the woman's legs. Her face was deep in concentration, gasping occasionally. The man's head rolled lewdly in the illuminated window, and both Julia and the priest stared into the distance as if all that was before them was darkness. The fear of being under surveillance mixed strangely with arousal, and as she felt compelled to leave the balcony and the company of the young priest, she also longed to stay, to simultaneously watch and be watched.

"We should go back in," she said again, turning away from the balcony. Behind her, she heard the young priest follow her into the apartment.

When they returned to the kitchen, Julia set the empty glass back on the table. Don Eugenio poured it full, then recorked the bottle and held it in his lap. Xabier looked to her as if to confirm that she had seen the man with the cigarette, and she nodded. But if Don Eugenio felt any regret at keeping this information from her, he didn't show it, as if he either expected that she had understood this all along or as if it simply had no bearing on her whatsoever.

"The phones?" Josu said, nodding toward the library where they had been earlier, where Julia had spoken to her parents that afternoon.

"Of course," Don Eugenio said. "There aren't many places they aren't listening these days."

The room was quiet for a moment, the significance of this information settling in.

"And what about you?" Josu said finally, turning his attention to Julia.

She didn't realize it then, but in this simple question the defense of ignorance that she didn't yet know she possessed was abruptly taken from her. She had gone from observer to participant in four words.

"What about her?" Xabier said. "Don Eugenio said she's OK. She's sympathetic."

"*Bai*," she said. It was the first Basque word she had ever learned, five summers before. *Yes*.

"Exactly," Josu said. He reached across the cutting board between them on the kitchen table and placed his hand on hers. "Don Eugenio trusts her. I trust her."

"I see," Don Eugenio said. "Yes, I think I see . . ."

"Sure," Xabier said. "That's an idea, isn't it?"

"It's worth discussing, anyway," Don Eugenio said. It seemed that Julia was the only one to not fully grasp the situation, but she resisted the urge to ask what they were talking about. To question their plans, she felt, would jeopardize her newly granted membership. "But first, one thing is certain—this will be your last meal for a while, no?"

Xabier nodded uncertainly.

"Well then, what would you like for your last supper?" the old man asked.

There was a pause, and for a moment only the sound of cold water could be heard rushing from the faucet. Don Eugenio and Julia turned to Xabier, but it was Josu that surprised her, standing suddenly.

"*Bacalao*," he said. He crossed the kitchen to where Lourdes stood, placing a hand on her waist. Julia could sense the calming gravity that his touch seemed to carry, the same sensation she had felt when standing beside him on the balcony earlier. "Would it be possible to prepare a *bacalao a la vizcaína*, Lourdes?"

"Of course, young man," Lourdes said. "Anything you'd like. And you too, Xabier." She paused for a second, the young priest's hand still casually on her waist. "What you're doing—it's something."

Don Eugenio nodded, sharing a look with Lourdes. Julia was beginning to understand their relationship in a different way, with a greater depth than she had first imagined. She had assumed Don Eugenio to be the intellectual and emotional center of the house, and that Lourdes was there only to serve and promote him in the patriarchal way that she took for granted as a part of the culture. But now she saw that they operated through one another, in tandem, in different ways but toward a common end. Lourdes patted Josu's hand, then turned to the refrigerator and began to remove paper bags filled with the tailings of green vegetables, a thick cut of white fish that Julia had bought for her at the market earlier in the day, wrapped in brown butcher paper.

"And you, young man?" she said across the kitchen to Xabier.

Xabier sat mutely for a moment, as if first considering what the following days might hold for him. The absence of food. The absence of taste.

"Come on, Xabi," Don Eugenio patted the young man on the back. "You're standing up to that *tocapelotas* Franco tomorrow," he said, borrowing the vulgarity Xabier had used earlier. "You'll need sustenance for your fight."

"All right," Xabier said. "I'm thinking."

"Anything you'd like."

"All right, all right," he said, then paused. He seemed to be gathering some of the bravado that he'd entered with. "A *chuleta*, please, Lourdes. A *chuleta* that just barely touches the frying pan. A *chuleta* so rare that it's still chewing its last meal."

"Bravo!" Don Eugenio said. "An excellent choice, Xabier."

"And you, Julia?" Josu said. "You'll join us, of course?"

And she thought this could mean several things at once, until Don Eugenio rose to help Lourdes at the kitchen counter.

"Of course," he said on her behalf. "Tonight, we all eat."

*

Forty minutes after leaving the university, Julia arrives to an empty house. Through a stand of pines she sees the lights of her neighbor's kitchen shining like yellow eyes, and for the first time since her divorce she feels an unease at the remoteness of the house on a dark country lane at the foothills of the Southern Cascades. It had rained earlier in the day, and the black leaves and pine needles still glisten.

Once inside, she quickly walks through the first floor of the house, turning on a light in each room. To combat the unsettling quiet, she turns on the television in the living room, an activity that she'd previously forbidden herself; the thought of watching television alone in the house has always seemed unbearably lonely and depressing, and so the set is only used when Katie and her grandchildren are home visiting. But now the blue glow of the screen seems comforting, the voices of television reporters filling the house.

Nearly every channel, of course, is occupied by banks of reporters and pundits. The defeated candidate was scheduled to appear on stage in New York City, at a convention center where Julia had once attended a book exposition, but the defeated candidate has cancelled her appearance. The evening's results had seemed so scripted, so preordained to Julia, that the evening is now imbued with the surreality of a dream, the real world tilted just a few degrees off-kilter. Even the moderators and pundits on the television seem unsettled, awkward silences creeping into their conversations. The outcome is so unexpected, the implications so unclear, that even these experts seem uncertain about what this might mean.

On a local news channel, a reporter is airing live from a protest that has broken out on Julia's campus. As the cameraman pans unsteadily across the front gates of the school, Julia sees a row of around thirty students locked arm-in-arm, obstructing the road. They are dressed almost entirely in black, their heads covered with hooded sweatshirts, dark bandanas hiding their faces. There is nothing to identify them, until Julia sits bolt upright on the couch. She notices a lock of dyed green hair hanging out from under a black hood, and she realizes that it must be the same young woman that spoke to her in the hall after class a couple of weeks before. The group approaches a police barricade, and the grey plume of a teargas canister fogs the camera's lens.

A few minutes later, the local news breaks coverage and a more polished national anchor takes over the screen. As she watches, Julia realizes, absently, that she hasn't eaten since lunch. She turns up the volume of the television, and the voices of the pundits follow her into the kitchen.

The refrigerator is depressingly bare, a fact that is ordinarily easy to ignore, but that only reinforces the isolation suddenly plaguing her. As a frozen organic lasagna spins in the microwave, the television breaks into a commercial for an American car company. For a moment, the name of the television star—whom the moderators have already begun, tentatively, to call the "president-elect,"—is absent, and in this absence Julia is reminded of the email that afternoon announcing the suicide of Xabier. She considers the depressing banality of her frozen meal, holds it up next to the memory of that last supper in Don Eugenio's apartment. *The Last Supper*. That's what Xabier had called it, in a letter sent from his mother's house in Sestao a decade after his release from prison. That's how it was with Xabier, his youthful humor long since supplanted with a bitter-edged irony.

As the microwave hums and the frozen meal revolves slowly on the glass carousel, Julia reconsiders the meal at Don Eugenio's, remembering her ignorance that night—all their ignorance. It had been such a small moment, a quotidian and necessary one, but also the beginning of the end of all things. In a glint, Julia wonders if this too might be such a moment, alone in her house on the night the television star is elected president—the beginning of the end of all things. The subversion, yet again, of the reality that she's constructed over a lifetime. For this one moment she exists, again, back in Don Eugenio's apartment with the two priests, the smell of fish and meat and cigarette smoke thick in her nostrils. All this in an instant, before the microwave beeps and the voices of the news anchors wend back into the house, and she is sucked back under by the tide of time.

*

After much lobbying by all four parties, Julia had settled on the *bacalao* with a generous wedge of *tortilla española* on the side—the tomato sauce from the fish should seep deliciously over into the potato omelet, she specified. For his part, Don Eugenio decided on rabbit cooked in a red wine reduction (which he had planned to eat that night anyway), while Lourdes chose only a sandwich of Iberian ham and smoked sheep's cheese, which the two priests set about preparing for her.

The three of them—Lourdes, Xabier, and Julia—worked together while Don Eugenio sipped from his wine glass and happily offered suggestions to the chefs. Josu, the somber young priest, shifted idly between the table and the counter, attempting awkwardly to pitch in before finally giving up and retreating to a wall near the table, where he moodily smoked cigarette after cigarette.

They laid nearly everything remaining from the refrigerator onto the kitchen counters before dividing up the tasks between them. Red chunks of rabbit that had been marinating since the night before were dredged through a bowl of flour, followed shortly thereafter by the two white cod fillets. Every iron skillet that had been stored under the oven was suddenly occupied, every saucepan bubbled with oil, chunks of meat, caramelizing onions. Don Eugenio was sent out to the corner bar to buy another two loaves of bread and returned twenty minutes later with the bread, an iced bottle of *sagardoa*, and a basket filled with golden *croquetas*. Oil from the fryer stained the napkins lining the basket, and his fingers shone with the grease.

"From Olatz," he said. "She insisted, and I'll admit I didn't put up much of a fight."

The room overflowed with competing senses: the foreign sound of Lourdes hooting at something Xabier had said, the sweetness of marrow and meat warming in a mixture of chicken stock and red table wine, an herbal freshness of chopped parsley and spent lemon wedges, Don Eugenio's long diatribe against the latest of the *Caudillo*'s abuses, a low hiss of gas as the oven roasted a plate of root vegetables, the familiar smell of fresh tomatoes being quartered and drizzled with olive oil and salt, a small applause when Lourdes flipped the heavy tortilla in a frying pan the size of a plate. Julia watched a saucepan steam with a dozen plum-colored mussels slowly opening in a broth of white wine, shallots, and butter, adding the briny smell of the sea to the room.

It was nearly one in the morning when Julia and the others sat down to the dinner table in the formal dining room, ravenous, leaving behind the kitchen strewn with potato peels and broken eggshells, plates caked with leftover flour and batters, and three empty bottles of Don Eugenio's best *reservas*. But before any of them picked up fork and knife they turned instinctively to Josu Juretegia—even his friend Xabier. Josu made the sign of the cross before beginning to recite the *Aita Gurea* in Basque.

> *Gure Aita, zeruetan zarena,*
> *santu izan bedi zure izena,*
> *etor bedi zure erreinua,*
> *egin bedi zure nahia,*
> *zeruan bezala lurrean ere.*
> *Emaiguzu gaur egun honetako ogia,*
> *barkatu gure zorrak,*
> *guk ere gure zordunei barkatzen diegunez gero;*
> *eta ez gu tentaldira eraman,*
> *baina atera gaitzazu gaitzetik.*

The fullness that had occupied the room for the last two hours seemed to vanish as the words were spoken, and Julia felt this warmth again replaced by the specter of Franco off in his palace in Madrid and his thugs hidden in the doorway across the street from Don Eugenio's apartment building. Even after the last mysterious words of that forbidden language were gone from the room, no one moved toward the dozen plates that were spread before them.

"I don't have to tell you the risk you're taking," Don Eugenio said. He was looking directly at Josu, who returned his stare. "You're familiar with this bishop. He could decide to make an example of you."

Josu shook his head with the certainty that all his physical gestures seemed to be imbued with.

"No," he said. "No, he won't do that."

"Not a chance," Xabier agreed. "He doesn't have the balls—excuse me for saying so, Lourdes. But it's true."

Don Eugenio brushed his palms across the chest of his sweater as he often did when preparing to address an audience, but before he had a chance to begin Josu spoke.

"Will—or *balls*—whatever you want to call it, has nothing to do with it. You're right, Don Eugenio. He has the will, and I don't doubt for a second that he'd make an example of us if he could. But I don't believe he has the capital right now. He's from another generation, Don Eugenio. He knows better than anyone that the next generation of our Church, men like Xabier and me, are not going to continue to tolerate the Church's support of the Regime. It's not worth it for him, Don Eugenio—he's not looking for a fight."

Josu spoke with a certainty that lent his words authority, and Julia could imagine the sermons he'd given since he'd left the seminary, the ones Don Eugenio said had already landed him in hot water with the bishop. He had meant to bring reassurance to their small group, and in a way he had. Don Eugenio reached across the table for the *bacalao a la vizcaína*, and Lourdes refilled her glass with cloudy yellow cider, and movement again spread through the room.

*

They ate slowly, Julia remembers, savoring the familiar flavors as if it were not just Josu and Xabier that did not know when they would eat again, but was the last meal for them all. They meditated on the saltiness of the bacalao, each sampling the flaky white fish slathered in sweet tomato sauce. They fetishized the perfect redness as Xabier cut into his steak and salivated over the oil and juice as it streamed out along the edge of the knife. They made note of the creaminess of the *croquetas*, the earthiness of the roasted roots, the tenderness of the rabbit's meat as it fell from the small lengths of bone. And when the meal was over, they celebrated the coolness of the custard inside the *tostadas* Lourdes brought out for dessert.

In between bites they drank. There was talk, followed by silence and then eventually by more discussion. They planned. They assumed responsibilities, made agreements. They colluded.

At one point Josu abruptly rose from the table and threw open the balcony windows onto the night sky. A chill entered the room as the smoke of a dozen cigarettes was carried out the window. Julia wondered if Josu was remembering the drunken couple in the apartment across the road, and if so, what it meant to him.

By the time they finished a second carafe of coffee, they had agreed upon the details of the plan. Don Eugenio would contact the local newspaper offices in person, to inform them about the nature of the priests' hunger strike. He would deliver a short manifesto that the priests had prepared, and he and Julia would keep tabs for the next several days to see if any of the papers were able to get the article past the censors. If, as they expected, the story was stopped before it made it to press, then this was where Julia would come in.

She had already purchased a return rail ticket that departed to Paris a week later. If the story of the priests' hunger strike had been suppressed in Spain, if their manifesto had not seen the light of day, then she was to take a copy of the manifesto to the offices of *Le Monde*, where a friend of Don Eugenio had ensured that it would be published. Upon her return to the university in Chicago, she would focus her efforts on bringing the world's attention to the plight of the Basque Country under Franco.

It was, as they reminded her, a simple plan.

*

Even now, as she flips through the television channels, each station preparing to broadcast the television star's victory speech, Julia finds herself believing in the simplicity of Josu and Xabier's plan, its viability, despite the disastrous series of events that unfolded from that night in Don Eugenio's apartment. She remembers Don Eugenio's description of Franco's ability to reach beyond the grave—back into the past and out into the future—and she is chilled by its clairvoyance.

Alone in her living room, the frozen lasagna barely disturbed, Julia allows her mind to wander, her imagination to take hold of history. If Xabier and Josu had shared the *Caudillo*'s powers of time travel, she thinks—those powers he had gained by slipping through cemeteries in darkness to scratch Basque surnames from headstones, by sneaking into hospital registries to change a generation of names to a bastardized Spanish version, by leaving a violent absence in the summer fiestas when people had once danced the *jota* or the *makildantza*, through torture and intimidation—when in time would Xabier Etxetoa and Josu Juretegia have traveled to, she wonders?

It's likely, she thinks, that the two young priests would have gone back to the days of the apostles, to mourn with them for the loss of their Messiah, to stand in solidarity against Pontius Pilate and to accept their punishment as penance, as they had been instructed since their childhoods. Or perhaps they would have gone back only a few hundred years, to blow out the lit pitch stick that had just been placed on the pyre set to immolate Joan of Arc in 1431, or two centuries later to the times of the Inquisition so that they might throw themselves at the feet of Phillip III in protest against the expulsion of the Jews and Moors from Spain.

Or instead, perhaps they might have journeyed *forward* in time from that night in Don Eugenio's apartment, she thinks. Perhaps they would have left the small safety of the kitchen warmed by the thick smells of *bacalao* and *chuleta* from Lourdes' stove, lit by the yellow incandescent bulb above the table, and instead ventured just a few days into the future, when the bishop of Bilbao began to tire of the publicity the young priests had gained by starving themselves on the front steps of his private residence.

If they had decided as much—to use the General's time machine to visit places in the future rather than the past—here's what Julia now knows they would have seen:

On the fifth day of their hunger strike the initial discomfort of starvation would have subsided and become familiar. The sips of water they allowed themselves would seem to provide sustenance enough for the day and the clarity of their cause would become even more apparent. In this near future they would have seen four Guardia Civiles part the small crowd that had gathered at the bishop's residence despite the universal silence of the local press, who were not able to slide the story past the *Caudillo*'s censors. Josu and Xabier would have seen the surprise on the faces of the crowd—as well as their own—as the officers hooked their arms around the shoulders of their future selves and dragged the two cassocked young men across the street and into the waiting police van.

Or they might have traveled to January of 1970, after they had each been found guilty of sedition and sentenced to twelve years in prison for the absurd act of spending several days in a public place without eating. They would hardly recognize themselves by this time, just a year and a half from that night at Don Eugenio's: their future selves would be gaunt, sallow from lack of sun. Xabier's youthful dark curls would have been cut close by the *Caudillo*'s barber, and the whiskers of his beard would have already begun to whiten from the stress of that first year.

And if they had spoken to these future selves, their future selves would have told them of the weeks in isolation. About how after a few days the silence of the cell gave way to a barrage of small sounds—the sound of a boot against a darkened hallway, of a spoon scraping the bottom of a soup bowl, of urine against the metal of the toilet—and about how these small sounds became deafening, suffocating. His future self would show Josu the small crescent of a cigarette burn on the inside of his forearm, the scarlet smudge of burst capillaries under his left eye.

If Xabier had spoken to his future self in 1974, he would have learned that entire weeks would pass without speaking to Josu, even though they were kept not only in the same prison barrack but just a few cells apart. He would discover that Josu no longer went to the morning mass offered at the prison, though it is doubtful that the Xabier of 1974 would tell his younger self of the targeted hit that Josu led on the prison yard against an inmate from Extremadura the week before Easter, or the flash of flesh that Xabier had once seen as Josu, the once-devout seminarian, pleasured himself with another prisoner in a darkened corner of their bunkhouse.

If they had used the *Caudillo*'s powers of time travel to visit the summer of 1976, the year after the *Caudillo*'s death (even the *Caudillo*, powerful *tocapelotas* that he was, wasn't powerful enough to escape death entirely), the young priests would find their future selves in separate places for the first time in eight years. Xabier would have found himself riding a train leaving from the prison in Zamora back to his hometown of Sestao, a grimy suburb of Bilbao, while his younger sister slept in the seat next to him with her head leaning against his shoulder, her dark ringlets standing out against his wiry white hair. When he returned home he would no longer be a member of the clergy, though he would still read each morning from the Bible that he was allowed to take from Zamora after he had accepted the clemency offered by the State—an uncharacteristic final gesture of kindness from the *Caudillo* after his death. (The *Caudillo*'s powers were enormous even in death, Don Eugenio noted during Julia's last visit with him in 1986, reaching beyond his undesecrated tomb in the *Valle de los Caídos* to inflict his will).

And Josu. In 1976, Julia thought, Josu would find himself still in prison, having refused the offer of mercy extended by the *Caudillo* and choosing instead to serve out the remaining four years of his sentence. Unlike Xabier, Josu's future self would no longer open his Bible each morning, as he had for the first twenty-seven years of his life. Instead, those readings would be replaced by meetings with other dissidents that had been sentenced to the prison. At these meetings he would exchange news about common friends with the other prisoners. He would discuss politics both inside and outside the concrete walls of Zamora. They would celebrate the latest assassination of the *Caudillo*'s men such as Luis Carrero Blanco, the named successor to the *Generalísimo* and next *tocapelotas* in line, whose car was thrown by an ETA bomb onto an apartment balcony five stories up. Remembering the letter she had received from him in January of 1977, Julia wonders if the younger Josu would be surprised to find himself at the table with three men conspiring to take revenge against the head guard at the prison (the one that had left the crescent-shaped scar on the inside of his arm), or if the Josu from that night at Don Eugenio's might have somehow divined all of this ahead of time and proceeded anyway.

As the television continues to flicker before her, Julia remembers another letter she'd once received from Josu, written in the summer after Xabier accepted the *Caudillo*'s pardon and was released from the prison. He'd ended the note with a quotation from *A Farewell to Arms*: "The world breaks everyone and afterward many are strong at the broken places. But those that will not break it kills." Alone with the voice of the television star, she turns the logic of this statement upside down, inside out. She seems to be able to apply it to either of the ex-priests in different iterations.

Julia begins to imagine the two young priests using the *Caudillo*'s mystical powers of time travel to arrive at *today*—at this night in November that finds her alone in her house in the woods, reminiscing about a dinner four decades in the past.

What then? What might they have said of her first brush with radicalism that August of 1968, when she had smuggled the two priests' short, romantic, ridiculous manifesto against the Church and the *Caudillo*'s regime across the border into France hidden in the folds of an old rain jacket in the suitcase that customs never checked? Would they be discouraged to know that when Julia delivered the manifesto to Don Eugenio's friend—the French newspaper editor—he only shrugged and flipped the pages onto his desk before asking her to dinner? That he never published a single word about Josu or Xabier or their manifesto or their twelve-year sentences?

What would they have thought of her now, alone in a comfortable home these forty years later, Julia wonders? Would they have approved of the career she had made out of Basque nationalism after that night in Bilbao, writing from the safety of an office in the back recesses of a university library?

But she had remained politically active in her own small ways, she told herself. She'd opposed the wars—all of them. Iraq I and II, Afghanistan, minor US involvement in the Balkans and northern Africa. In the years since Bilbao, she'd been maced, had been detained and arrested, had written articles and led rallies—activities that landed her on the cover of the school newspaper and in front of disciplinary committees, and finally even won her a tenured faculty position.

*

And most importantly, Julia wonders: if they were to use the *Caudillo*'s time machine to suddenly arrive at *tonight*—as the pundits ready themselves for the television star's acceptance speech—what would the two young priests think of their future selves, of where their own lives have landed?

In order to find himself today, Josu would be required not only to travel through forty-five years of history, past the deaths of dictators and the opening of prison doors and the explosions of primers in brass bullet casings, but also across four thousand four hundred eighty miles of ocean to a two-story house on a side street off Avenida Camilo Cienfuegos in a suburb of Havana, Cuba. He would find himself alone in a room filled with orderly stacks of books and papers, handwritten drafts of articles and lectures written over thirty years in exile. He would have been recaptured in southern France in 1984, then deported to Panama, which subsequently agreed to send him and eight other radicals—who had by then been deemed "terrorists"—to Cuba on the condition that they agree never to return to Europe. The young Josu would find his future self shorter, stooped in a way that all men become if they are lucky enough to reach that age. He would be tanned and well-fed. He would find himself godless but not unhappy, the father of a daughter who is a doctor at the Hospital Miguel Enríquez and a son who drives taxi and has two children of his own.

Julia remembers the last time she saw Josu in person, in Cuba, thirty years after their first meeting. It was six months after her divorce, and she'd used a conference in Havana as an excuse to make the trip. They'd returned to her hotel room after dinner, something that each had seemed to expect from the outset. Josu had turned the lights off in the room before finally touching her, as if he were trying to recall her from thirty years before, the way she existed on that balcony at Don Eugenio's, trying to imagine away three decades of life. It was, in all senses, anticlimactic, the ex-priest going soft after a couple of minutes, apologizing to Julia as she pulled her hands back through the sleeves of her blouse.

And Xabier. It's likely that he would be even more surprised by where he would find himself in the hours before his death, she thinks, had he been blessed with the *Caudillo*'s powers of time travel. When Julia recalls Xabier from that dinner at Don Eugenio's—his last meal as the man that existed before prison—she remembers him as another person entirely: a jokester, the more immature of the two young priests. This young version of Xabier is, for her, almost irreconcilable with the man that she found during her trip to the Basque Country earlier this year, back when the television star had been only a late-night comic's joke, only a vulgar distraction during the early campaign season.

If his younger self were to find Xabier in the last days before taking his own life, Julia is certain that he would be horrified not only by the effects of time, but also by the booming repercussions of that small act of protest, the hunger strike at the bishop's residence. He would see just how profoundly he had been changed not only by his years in prison, but by the dissociation he had felt upon his return to Sestao. He would find himself unskilled, unable to practice the vocation conferred by several years at the seminary. He would have never married. He would have had jobs here and there, been forced to apply for government assistance when he was out of work, to borrow money from his mother and his sister.

His future self would still be a man of faith, Xabier may have been surprised to find, though this faith would have an emptiness at its core, a loneliness that he could not unknow and that informed every day, every action until his death. Alone in her living room, Julia thinks back to a conversation that she had with Xabier in a café in Bilbao, after Franco had died and Xabier had accepted the *Caudillo*'s pardon from beyond the grave.

"In prison, I showed the doctor these burns," he said, pulling back his sleeve to reveal a series of ugly keloid scars, each four inches across. "They are from a wire hanger that the guards heated on a stovetop." He'd looked at the floor, avoiding her eyes. "There are others like these on the bottoms of my feet."

"I'm sorry," Julia had said. Xabier shook his head, as if she were missing the point.

"Do you know what the doctor said when I showed him the burns?"

"No," Julia said.

"He told me, 'I don't see any burns,' " Xabier said. When Xabier looked at her, his eyes were red and glassy. "He even put his hands on the burns, on the place where I *thought* the burns were. And then he just shrugged and said again, 'I don't see any burns. Everything here is perfectly normal.' "

Later that day he had asked Josu about it, Xabier told her. "I was afraid I was losing my mind, that I really hadn't been burned."

When Xabier showed him the burns, Josu stood silent, trembling with anger, before dropping on a knee next to him on the prison bench. Josu reached over and brought near a tin that he had been drinking from, and he poured the water carefully over the scars on Xabier's feet.

"I found myself crying, in a way I hadn't since my first day in the prison," Xabier said. At the table next to them in the café, a group of old women gossiped idly over a game of *mus*.

" 'You aren't losing your mind, Xabier,' Josu told me. 'The burns are there. They are real.' "

When Xabier turned towards her, Julia found herself picking up her spoon, stirring her coffee nervously. She was afraid to look him in the eyes.

"Josu finished pouring the water on my feet, and began to dry them with a shirt that was on the bench. 'But now,' he told me," Xabier's words were a shaking whisper, barely audible in the noisy café. " '*Now* they are gone.' "

*

It is late—past midnight on the West Coast—when the television star takes the stage. The cameras pan across the audience in New York, and the television star's supporters shake with a celebration that seems to Julia to border on rage. None of the signs that the audience hold up have the name of the television star's political party, she notices. Just the name. Just the name. She is reminded of the man that had harassed her at the stoplight earlier in the night, and she realizes now that this man, and others like him, now control her country.

As the television star speaks, Julia hears the words of Franco, the Great Ventriloquist, as Don Eugenio had called him, coming through the television star's mouth. It occurs to her, for the first time, that Franco himself might not have been the Great Ventriloquist after all. That he—like all the other great ventriloquists of the twentieth century—might have been merely a mouthpiece for something else. God, or godlessness, or the atomic bomb, or simply modernity. The great dark powers that upend reality, that travel through time and strike down people like Josu and Xabier. She remembers the call from Katie earlier that evening from New York, and she herself, for the first time, feels the sudden vulnerability that the two priests must have felt that morning in Bilbao when the *Caudillo*'s men dragged them into the police van.

On the screen in her living room, the television star has stopped speaking for a moment, and merely stands at a lectern while the crowd in the auditorium cheers. Men wave blue flags and placards with the television star's name on them. When the camera lens lands on him, there is something inexplicable about the television star that suggests he knows nothing and yet, simultaneously, knows everything. It chills her in an ephemeral, almost supernatural way, as if she were in the presence of the great pagan wizards and witches that were said to inhabit the medieval Basque countryside.

Incongruously, as the television star speaks to her through the flat screen television, the smells of that final dinner at Don Eugenio's forty years ago return to her in the dim emptiness of her house in the woods. She tastes the sweet glaze of caramelized pepper and olive oil at the corners of her lips, and she suddenly remembers the moment on Don Eugenio's balcony when she and Josu had watched the neighbor's head rolling in his lover's lap, her mouth open in an ecstasy muted by the closed apartment windows.

She thinks of the girl with the green hair that she'd recognized on television earlier that night, and of her daughter in New York, just miles away from the television star's victory party. Her grandchildren. What decision would *she* have made, Julia now wonders, if she had been given access to the General's time machine? If she had been able to travel forward—forward to the present—and then back to that night in Don Eugenio's, before it was too late? She recalls a moment in the old professor's apartment that night, when the heavy warmth of the meal was still present in the dining room and Xabier had fallen asleep in his chair while Josu sipped cautiously, meditatively at a second cup of coffee, and Don Eugenio and Lourdes shared a look suggesting they were the only people in the world who understood the importance of this quiet moment.

Would she have allowed it all to happen?

What then? What now?

####

www.ingramcontent.com/pod-product-compliance
Lightning Source LLC
LaVergne TN
LVHW051018080826
845145LV00009B/2692

9781949805581